DAD, JACKIE, and ME

MYRON UHLBERG

ILLUSTRATED BY

COLIN BOOTMAN

Ω

PEACHTREE

ATLANTA

My ear was glued to the radio, like every other ear in Brooklyn.

It was Opening Day, 1947. And every kid in Brooklyn knew this was our year.

The Dodgers were going to go all the way!

We had Jackie Robinson, the first Negro player in major league baseball.

As I listened to the game, the minutes melted into hours; the innings folded one into another. I could see it all in my mind's eye: pitch after pitch, swing after swing. I dreamed of the day I could see it all for myself.

Our neighborhood was only a short subway ride from Ebbets Field, home of the Dodgers and their new first baseman.

I loved baseball. I loved the Brooklyn Dodgers. I hated the New York Giants, and they hated Jackie Robinson.

One day, my father came home early from work. He walked into my bedroom and announced, "We're going to Ebbets Field."

He didn't say it out loud. My father was deaf, so he signed the words with his hands.

I couldn't believe it. Dad had never seemed to care much about baseball.

"I want to meet Jackie Robinson," Dad signed.

I was finally going to see a real game. Today the Dodgers were playing the Giants.
And we were going to cream 'em.

I got my glove and ball, Dodgers cap, and scorecard. I stuck my lucky pencil
behind my ear. As we went down the steps, I tossed the ball to Dad. But he'd never
played baseball like me. He dropped it.

I couldn't wait to get to the ballpark. But the whole ride I kept thinking, There's no way Dad can meet Jackie Robinson. Besides, Jackie doesn't know sign language.

How would they talk to each other?

The line to get in to Ebbets Field snaked around Sullivan Place and up to Bedford Avenue. My dad let me hold my ticket. I clutched it for dear life.

Finally, we were through the turnstile. My dad held my hand as we moved with the rest of the crowd through the gloomy underbelly of the stadium, up the dark ramp. Then we tumbled into bright sunlight.

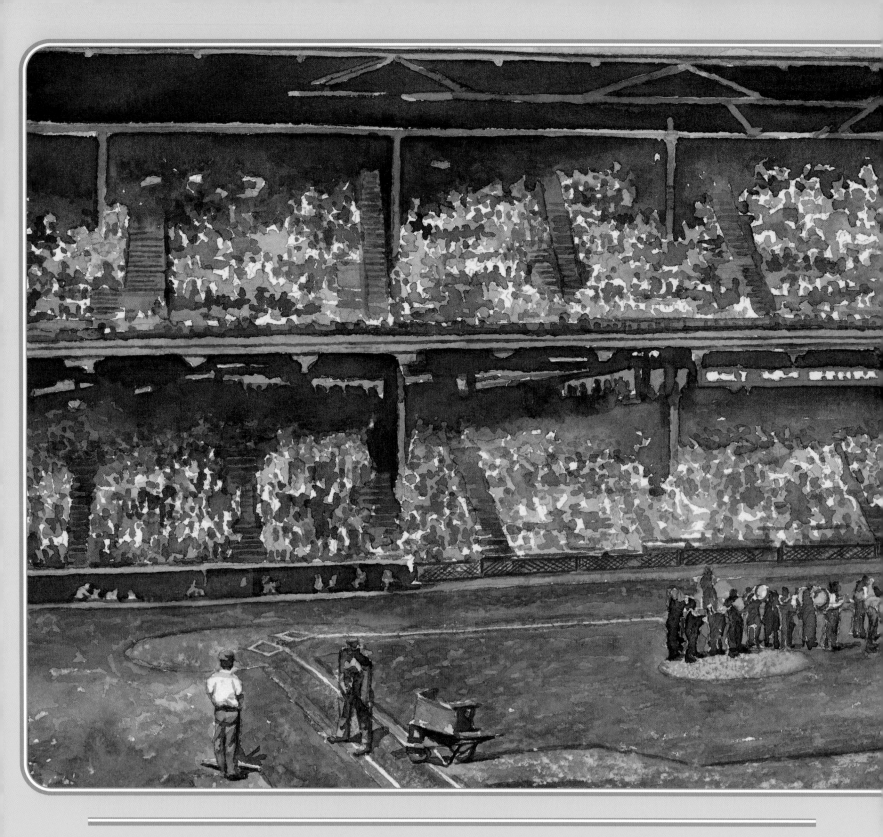

I shut my eyes against the glare. When I opened them again, my breath caught in my throat. I had never seen anything so perfect as the inside of Ebbets Field.

There, laid out at my feet, was the emerald green field, each blade of grass reflecting the light from the afternoon sun.

The angles of the field were sharply marked in two lines of white chalk.

The dirt base paths formed a perfect diamond carpet dotted with fat canvas bags at each base and a black rubber plate at home.

I knew if I lived to be a hundred, I would never again see a sight so beautiful.

"Hey, peanuts! Hey, hot dogs! Get 'em while they're hot!"

Dad and I sat on the right field line, right behind first base, Jackie's position.

The Dodgers Sym-Phony was marching up and down the aisles playing "The Worms Crawl In, the Worms Crawl Out." The music was earsplitting. Dad couldn't hear it, but he laughed along with everyone else at the sight of the raggedy band's tattered clothes, cowbells and whistles.

When the game started and Jackie ran out on the field, Dad yelled real loud, "Jackiee, Jackiee, Jackiee!" Only it didn't come out that way. It sounded like, "AH-GHEE, AH-GHEE, AH-GHEE!" Since my dad couldn't hear, he had no way of knowing what the words should sound like.

Everyone looked at my dad.

I looked at my shoes.

As Jackie stood at first base, the Giants began hooting and hollering. They called Jackie names. Horrible names. "What are they saying?" Dad asked.

"Bad things," I said.

"Tell me." Some of those words I had to finger spell. I knew no sign for them.

Dad listened with a sad little smile on his face.

In the ninth inning, Jackie bunted, and beat the throw to first. Then he stole second.

On the next Dodgers hit, he moved to third. The score was tied at four–all.

The Giants pitcher took a long windup, and Jackie dashed for home. We all jumped to our feet yelling, "Jackiee, Jackiee, Jackiee!"

"AH-GHEE, AH-GHEE, AH-GHEE!" Dad screamed.

This time, nobody seemed to notice.

The heck with the Giants. They were nothing! We had Jackie Robinson.

Every day when Dad came home from work, he started asking me questions. Not about school. About baseball. He wanted to know everything I knew. Especially about Jackie Robinson.

"What's Jackie's batting average?"

".247," I said.

"How's that figured?"

I explained.

"What's an RBI?" he asked.

"Runs batted in."

"Fielding average. What's that mean?"

I told him.

"You teach me baseball," he signed.

"Okay," I said.

One night, Dad came home with a baseball glove.

"Let's have a catch," he signed.

We tossed the ball back and forth until Mom called us for supper. Dad missed the ball every time. The only way he could hold it was by trapping the ball against his chest with both hands. That had to hurt, but Dad just smiled.

"Jackie never drops the ball," he signed. "He catches it with one hand. Not like me."

All that week we practiced. Dad dropped the ball most every time. Even when I threw it underhand.

"Throw it regular," Dad said.

Dad and I kept going to games whenever we could. Every time Jackie came out to his position, Dad chanted right along with the crowd. AH-GHEE, AH-GHEE, AH-GHEE.

Jackie never looked over at us. He just stared down the line at the next hitter.

One Sunday, the Dodgers were playing the St. Louis Cardinals. What a game! Our pitcher had a no-hitter going.

And then it happened. On a simple grounder that he knew he couldn't beat, a Cardinal player crossed first base and spiked Jackie—on purpose! Fifty-two thousand eyes popped. Twenty-six thousand jaws dropped. Twenty-six thousand tongues were stilled.

Then, in that awful silence, my father jumped to his feet.

"NOOOO!" he screamed. "NOT FAIR! AH-GHEE, AH-GHEE, AH-GHEE!"

The Brooklyn crowd went nuts. They leapt to their feet and joined my father.

"JACK-IE, JACK-IE, JACK-IE!"

The name bounced off the brick walls, climbed the iron girders, and rattled around under the wooden roof.

But Jackie just stood at first base, his face a blank mask, blood streaming down his leg. It was almost as if he didn't hear the crowd.

All that month, Dad and I followed everything Jackie did. We read and reread every report of every game that was printed in *The New York Daily News.*

Dad started a scrapbook. If there was any mention of Jackie Robinson, he cut out the article and pasted it in his scrapbook.

The scrapbook got thicker.

The Dodgers kept winning.

And the opposing teams kept riding Jackie Robinson.

But Jackie never reacted. He didn't even seem to notice. And he never complained.

The Dodgers clinched the pennant that season when the Cards beat the Cubs.

Dad and I went downtown the next day to see the big parade to honor Jackie.

And back in the neighborhood, we had a block party to celebrate.

It didn't matter whether the Dodgers won the last game of the season, since we were already over the top. But Dad and I didn't care. We went to Ebbets Field anyway. We went to see Jackie Robinson.

In the third inning, Jackie smacked the ball to deep left field for a double. Then he flew home like the wind, his feet barely touching the base path.

The Brooklyn crowd went crazy. "Go, Go, Go, Jackieeee!"

"GOO, GOO, GOO, AH-GHEEEE!" my dad screamed right along with them.

Finally, late in the day, as deep shadows stretched across the infield, Jackie caught a line drive hit down the first base line. It was the last out of the game.

As the crowd cheered, Jackie stood alone at first base, staring at the ball in his glove.

Then he turned and threw it into the stands—right to my father!

That's when my dad did something he had never done before. He reached up and caught the ball in his bare hand!

I'm not sure, but I think I saw Jackie Robinson smile. My dad dropped the ball into my empty glove.

And just like that, the baseball season of 1947 was over.

Author's Note

This story is a work of fiction. Parts of it, however, are based in truth.

My father, who was deaf and spoke only with his hands, worked as a printer for *The New York Daily News*. One night in 1947, he brought home the paper—the ink not quite dry—and excitedly showed me the bold headline: BROOKLYN DODGERS SIGN JACKIE ROBINSON. Beneath it was a photo of two smiling men: the president of the Brooklyn Dodgers, Branch Rickey, and the grandson of a slave, Jackie Robinson.

"Now, at last," my father signed to me, "a Negro will play in the major leagues!"

And from the day he joined the Brooklyn Dodgers until the day he retired, Jackie Robinson was the main topic of conversation in our small Brooklyn apartment during every baseball season.

My father could not throw or catch a baseball, let alone hit one. As a boy in 1910, he attended a deaf residential school, where playing sports was not encouraged. In those days most people considered deaf children severely handicapped and thought teaching them sports a waste of time. What could my deaf father possibly have in common with this Negro baseball player, Jackie Robinson?

During Jackie's first year as a Dodger, my father took me to many games. He told me to watch carefully how the opposing team would single Jackie out for unfair treatment, how they would actively discriminate against him on the field just because his skin was brown. "Just you watch," he said. "Jackie will show them that his skin color has nothing to do with how he plays baseball. He will show them all that he is as good as they are."

Throughout his life my father also experienced the cruelty of prejudice. "It's not fair that hearing people discriminate against me just because I am deaf," he told me. "It doesn't matter, though," he always added. "I show them every day I am as good as they are."

One summer day, late in that rookie season of 1947—during which Jackie had quietly endured racial taunts, threats on his life, numerous bean balls, and even deliberate spikings—my father told me about another hero.

"There was a deaf man born in 1862," he signed to me, "who was also a baseball player. His name was William Ellsworth Hoy, but his teammates quickly nicknamed him 'The Amazing Dummy.'

"In those days no one could imagine that a deaf man could play major league baseball. The deaf were thoughtlessly called 'deaf and dumb.' It was common for the hearing to refer to a deaf person as a 'dummy.'

"But Dummy Hoy showed them all," my father continued. "He played fourteen years in the major leagues. He was smart and fast like Jackie, and in his rookie year he stole a record eighty-two bases. One day, he threw three men out at home plate from the outfield, which had never been done before. And, most importantly, he taught umpires to use hand signals to call balls and strikes."

As he told that story, I began to understand the connection between Jackie Robinson and my deaf father. Like Dummy Hoy before them, they were both men who worked to overcome thoughtless prejudice and to prove themselves every day of their lives.

—M.U.

Dedication

This book is dedicated in loving memory to Bob Domozych:
Brooklyn boy, Dodger fan, Brandeis pioneer, and above all, my great,
irreplaceable friend. And to my wife, Karen, with love, as always.

—*M. U.*

I dedicate this book to Brooklyn and all baseball lovers.

—*C. B.*

Acknowledgments

Special thanks to Sarah Helyar Smith, who first encouraged me to write about my deaf father and his emotional connection to the great Jackie Robinson; to Lisa Banim, whose sensitive editing helped me rethink and reshape the story; to Loraine Joyner, who transformed my words into an eye-popping book; to Margaret Quinlin, my dear steadfast friend, who was the first to give me permission to be a writer and is always ready with wise counsel; and to all the rest of the amazing Peachtree family.

I am also grateful to Francine I. Henderson, Research Administrator of the Auburn Avenue Research Library on African-American Culture and History in Atlanta, GA; the National Baseball Hall of Fame and Museum in Cooperstown, NY; and to Margot Hayward, Brooklynite and Brooklyn Dodgers fan extraordinaire, for help in authenticating the setting for this story.

Published By

Ω

Peachtree Publishers
1700 Chattahoochee Avenue   Atlanta, Georgia 30318-2112
www.peachtree-online.com

Text © 2005 by Myron Uhlberg
Illustrations © 2005 by Colin Bootman

First trade paperback edition published in January 2010

Illustrations created in watercolor on Arches Aquarelle 100% rag paper. Scrapbook-page endpapers courtesy of Margot Hayward from her private collection. Text typeset in FontShop International's FF Acanthus; headings and large capitals typeset in SWFTE International's Gravure; title created with Adobe Charcoal.

Book design by Loraine M. Joyner

10 (hardcover)
10 9 8 7 (trade paperback)

Printed in the United States in March 2016 by Worzalla in Stevens Point, Wisconsin

Library of Congress Cataloging-in-Publication Data

Uhlberg, Myron.
   Dad, Jackie, and me / written by Myron Uhlberg ; illustrated by Colin Bootman.— 1st ed.
      p. cm.
Summary: In Brooklyn, New York, in 1947, a boy learns about discrimination and tolerance as he and his deaf father share their enthusiasm over baseball and the Dodgers' first baseman, Jackie Robinson.
   ISBN 978-1-56145-329-0 (hardcover)
   ISBN 978-1-56145-531-7 (trade paperback)
[1. Baseball—Fiction. 2. Deaf—Fiction. 3. Toleration—Fiction. 4. Robinson, Jackie, 1919-1972—Fiction. 5. Brooklyn Dodgers (Baseball team)—Fiction. 6. Brooklyn (New York, N.Y.)—History—20th century—Fiction.] I. Bootman, Colin, ill. II. Title.

PZ7.U3257Dad 2005
[Fic]—dc22
2004016711